ALEXANDER FOX
AND THE
AMAZING MIND READER

D0057284

ALEXANDER FOX AND THE AMAZING MIND READER

John C. Clayton

 Prometheus Books

59 John Glenn Drive
Amherst, NewYork 14228-2197

Published 1998 by Prometheus Books

02 01 00 99 98   5 4 3 2 1

Library of Congress Cataloging-in-Publication Data

Clayton, John C.
    Alexander Fox & the amazing mind reader / John C. Clayton ; illustrated by Emily Egan.
        p.   cm.
    Summary: At the request of a classmate, sixth grader and scientific investigator Alex Fox probes the mystery of a so-called psychic who claims to read minds and find missing objects.
    ISBN 1–57392–221–8 (pbk.)
    [1. Extrasensory perception—Fiction. 2. Mystery and detective stories.] I. Egan, Emily, ill. II. Title.
PZ7.C57918Al   1998
[Fic]—dc21   98–4379
                                                                        CIP
                                                                         AC

Printed in the United States of America on acid-free paper.

For my dad and mom.

Alexander Fox was surprised to see one of the Fitz-water kids walking toward his table.

The Fitzwater family was rich, and the three kids acted like it. Usually they didn't even look at you when they passed you in the hallway. They just looked right past you as if you didn't exist—or didn't matter. But here was Spencer Fitzwater, looking Alex straight in the eye and walking up as if he actually planned to talk to Alex.

Alex put his milk carton back on the tray and waited curiously to see what, if anything, Fitzwater might have to say.

Fitzwater leaned across the lunchroom table. "You're the kid who doesn't believe anything, right?" he said.

Alex grinned. It looked like he was starting to get a reputation around school. "I believe a lot of things," he said. "But for certain things, I expect to see real proof first."

Fitzwater looked puzzled. "What do you mean?"

"Unusual claims require unusually strong evidence," Alex said.

Fitzwater had an odd look on his face, as if he had no clue what Alex was talking about. Alex figured he'd better try to explain.

"Let's say that you tell me you were just outside and you saw a car," Alex said. "I'd probably believe you because seeing cars is nothing unusual."

"Big deal," Fitzwater said.

"Let me finish," Alex said. "Now let's suppose that you tell me you were just outside and you saw a flying saucer."

"A flying saucer?" Fitzwater said.

"That's a pretty unusual thing to claim, isn't it?" Alex asked. "If you want me to believe something like that, you have to give me proof. Real solid proof. Not blurry photos of something that could be a plain old hubcap on a string."

"Well, what if I didn't happen to have my camera with me at the time?" Fitzwater asked.

Alex shrugged. "Then come back when you do have proof. I'm not going to waste my time believing in things like flying saucers, unicorns, or mermaids unless I have good reason to believe."

"Well, I didn't come over here to talk about mermaids," said Fitzwater, putting his fists on his hips. "I came over to tell you that *I* know a real psychic. How do you like *that*?"

"A psychic?" Alex said.

Fitzwater could no doubt hear the skeptical tone in Alex's voice. "This guy's the real thing," Fitzwater insisted. "He can find lost objects. He can predict the future. He can even read minds."

"Have you actually seen him do this stuff?" Alex asked. He knew that sometimes people hear stories like this, and they believe them, even though they haven't actually seen anything with their own eyes.

Fitzwater nodded excitedly. "He's done it right in my own house. He found my mom's missing watch. He read my mind. The guy's incredible!"

"*Incredible* is the word, all right," Alex said. "Mind if I investigate?"

"Investigate?" said Fitzwater, puzzled.

Alex fished around in his shirt pocket and then presented his business card.

Fitzwater read the card curiously. "'Alexander Fox, scientific investigator'?"

"Scientists look for proof," Alex said. "Let's investigate and see if we can prove that this guy has real psychic powers."

Alex had no idea he would soon witness things that would amaze even him.

“Now, let me get this straight,” Fitzwater said, leaning back in the soft cushions of the sofa. “I don’t have to pay you for this so-called investigation, right?”

They were sitting in the Foxes’ family room. Alex’s sister, Teri, and his friend Jay Hong had joined them there after school. Jay was in the sixth grade with Alex. Teri was in the seventh grade. They all went to the same school.

Alex included Jay and Teri in all of his big cases. He liked to tell people that Jay and Teri were his “business associates.” Teri felt that should entitle them to business cards like Alex’s, but she hadn’t been able to convince Alex of that yet.

"I won't charge you a dime," Alex assured Fitzwater. "I'm only interested in finding the truth. After all, if this guy really can read minds and see into the future, this will be one of the greatest discoveries of all time."

"He can," Fitzwater insisted. "I've seen him do it."

"Well, let's start at the beginning," Alex said, flipping open the spiral notebook that he used for all of his investigations. "First, what's this guy's name?"

"Arcady Mystikos," Fitzwater said.

Alex peered over the top of his notebook.

Fitzwater looked dead serious.

"Arcady Mystikos," Alex repeated.

Fitzwater spelled it for him, and Alex wrote it down.

"That's quite a name," he said.

"He's from Greece," Fitzwater explained. "He has an accent, but he speaks English well."

"I see," Alex said, adding this information to his notes. "And when did you first meet this Mr. Mystikos?"

"It was about a week ago," Fitzwater said. "My mother was giving a party for some friends."

"And your mother invited him?" Alex asked.

"No, I think Mrs. Winslow brought him along as her guest," Fitzwater said.

"This Mrs. Winslow is a friend of your mother's?" Alex asked.

Fitzwater nodded. "She knew that my mother was looking for a reliable psychic, so she brought Mr. Mystikos along."

"And how did Mrs. Winslow first meet Mr. Mystikos?" Alex asked.

Fitzwater shrugged. "I dunno. She knows all the big psychics. She's very curious about things like ESP – you know, extrasensory perception."

"Mrs. Winslow spends a lot of money on that kind of stuff?" Alex asked.

Fitzwater shrugged again. "You'd have to ask her. I do know that she can afford it. She's got even more money than *my* family."

Alex decided to ignore that last comment, but he could see that Teri was clenching her fists. Teri didn't appreciate snobs. Alex hoped there wouldn't be any trouble. After all, Teri had a brown belt in judo. It wouldn't look very good if Teri beat up the person who had given them this case.

"So, Mrs. Winslow introduced Mr. Mystikos to your mother at this party," Alex said.

Fitzwater nodded.

"And then what happened?" Alex asked.

Fitzwater leaned forward. "Right away, he knew all kinds of stuff about my mother," he said excitedly. "All he had to do was touch her hand, and he could sense all these things about her. He knew how many kids she had and what kind of car she drove and even that she liked to play tennis. He knew everything!"

"He knew how many kids your mom has," Alex said. "Could Mrs. Winslow have told him that?"

Fitzwater shrugged. "I guess so, but..."

"Were you and your brothers there at the party?" Alex asked.

"Yeah."

"So he could have seen the three of you with his own eyes," Alex pointed out.

"Yeah, but..."

"What about tennis trophies?" Alex asked. "Does your mother keep anything like that around the house?"

"In the study," Fitzwater said. "She keeps them in a glass case."

"Maybe that's how he knew that she likes to play tennis," Alex said. "Or maybe Mrs. Winslow told him. What about your mom's car? Could Mr. Mystikos have peeked in the garage at some point?"

"I dunno," Fitzwater said, sounding like he was about to get angry. "I'll admit that some of this stuff anybody could find out. But he could do all kinds of amazing things!"

"Like what?" Alex asked.

"Like reading my mind," Fitzwater said.

"Go on," Alex said, ready to take more notes.

"He told my mother that he could sense people's thoughts," Fitzwater said. "To prove it, he asked me to write down a number between one and a hundred. Then he told me what it was!"

"Wow!" Teri said.

Alex gave his sister a disapproving look. Teri tended to be a little less skeptical than Alex would have liked. They had both inherited their mother's red hair, but only Alex had inherited his mother's interest in science and investigation. Mrs. Fox taught physics and chemistry at a local high school.

Teri was more like their father when it came to

believing in unproven things like ghosts and ESP. For instance, Teri believed that one of her goldfish had psychic powers because it swam to the top of the bowl every time she went to feed it.

"What did you write this number on?" Alex asked.

Fitzwater thought a moment. "Just some notepad."

"Was it your notepad or did Mr. Mystikos bring it with him?" Alex asked.

"I dunno," Fitzwater said.

Alex was not surprised. He had found that people usually did not have a very clear memory of events like this. They remembered the big, impressive stuff, but forgot the small details that sometimes help an investigator explain things later.

"Try to remember," Alex urged him.

"I think he brought it with him," Fitzwater said. "Yeah, I think he pulled it out of his jacket pocket."

"What did you do with this piece of paper after you wrote the number on it?" Alex asked.

"I put it in an envelope."

"Mr. Mystikos told you to do this?" Alex asked.

Fitzwater nodded.

"What did you do next?" Alex asked.

"I sealed the envelope, and he guessed the number without even opening it," Fitzwater said.

"Who was holding the envelope?" Alex asked.

"Me," Fitzwater said proudly, as if he had just proved that there was no trickery involved.

"And who had the notepad?" Alex asked.

Fitzwater shrugged. "Who knows? Who cares? I was done with the notepad at that point."

"I just want to make sure there was no way for this guy to cheat," Alex said.

"Look," Fitzwater said angrily. "This wasn't some stupid magic trick. This guy really has psychic powers. He found my mom's missing watch!"

Alex flipped to a new page in his notebook. "How long had the watch been missing?" he asked.

"She had it on when the party started, but then it disappeared, and she couldn't find it anywhere," Fitzwater said. "And that's a very expensive watch."

Alex glanced at Spencer Fitzwater's own gold watch. "I'm sure it is," he said without further comment.

"Well, naturally my mom got all upset," Fitzwater said. "But then Mr. Mystikos assured her that he could find it. And he did."

"How did he do that?" Alex asked.

"He asked if he could hold something else that belonged to my mom. She gave him one of her rings. Then he just sort of wandered around the house, holding the ring and mumbling to himself."

"And where did he find her watch?" Alex asked.

"You'd never guess," Fitzwater said. "It was in a flowerpot! My mother has no idea how it got there. Mr. Mystikos says that strange things tend to happen whenever he's around. He thinks small

objects get moved from one place to another by some kind of weird psychic energy that surrounds him."

"That's a pretty wild claim," Alex said. "Do you think there might be other possible explanations?"

"Like what?" Fitzwater said defiantly. "Are you going to tell me that Mr. Mystikos stole my mother's watch and hid it in that flowerpot?"

"We certainly can't rule that out yet," Alex said. "And it would fit the facts."

"Look," Fitzwater said, standing up suddenly. "Maybe I'm just wasting my time here. You obviously don't want to believe that any of this could really happen."

"I'm willing to believe *all* of it," Alex corrected him, "once we have proof."

"Alex can be a bit skeptical," Teri told Fitzwater.

Alex gave her a dirty look. He and Teri had been having this same argument for months.

"There's nothing wrong with being skeptical," he told her for the umpteenth time.

"You're just not willing to believe," she told him. "There are a lot of things in this universe that science cannot explain. Do you think it's impossible for some people to have amazing mental powers that the rest of us don't?"

"I never said anything was impossible," he said. "I just think that we shouldn't jump to conclusions. Let's rule out all the likely explanations first before we start believing in the unlikely ones."

Alex noticed that Fitzwater had moved over next to Teri. They were both staring at Alex with their hands on their hips. It looked like they were teaming up against him. It was the believers against the skeptic. Alex glanced over at his trusty friend Jay.

Jay's head was tilted back against the sofa, and his mouth was wide open. Jay was sound asleep.

Irritated, Alex nudged Jay with his toe.

Jay opened his eyes with a start. "Huh?" he said. "What's going on?"

"Alex is being stubborn again," Teri told him.

"So what else is new?" Jay asked.

"Look," Alex said, trying not to sound mad. "Spencer hasn't told me one thing about this Mr. Mystikos that couldn't be done by a good cheat. I want proof that this guy really has some kind of amazing power."

"Alex!" called a voice from upstairs. "Phone!"

It was his mother.

"Mom, I'm busy!" Alex yelled back. "I'm working on a case!"

"He says it's important," she said, appearing in the doorway. "He says he has to talk to you right away."

Alex shot an irritated glance up the stairs. "Who is it?" he asked.

"He sounds foreign," replied his mother. "He says his name is Mr. Mystikos."

A lex looked at Teri. Teri looked at Alex. A cold tingle ran down Alex's back.

"Are you going to answer it?" Teri asked him in a cautious whisper.

Alex hesitated. "I guess I have to."

"Oh, great," Fitzwater said, throwing his hands in the air. "He knows we're here! He knows we've been talking about him!"

"Let's not jump to conclusions," Alex said, fighting off his own worries. "We need more information. I'll go talk to him."

He started toward the stairs. Everybody followed him. They tromped up the wooden stairs together.

Alex's mom handed him the phone and then stood there, waiting. Apparently, she was curious about this call, too.

"Hello," Alex said. "This is..."

"You do not have to tell me," said a deep voice with a strong accent. "You are Alexander Fox. I see two words. One word begins with the letter *S*. *Science*, I think. Or *scientific*. Yes, that is it. The other word is a long one. *Inventions?* No. *Investigator!* 'Scientific investigator.' That is what you call yourself, no?"

"That's right," Alex said uneasily. He exchanged glances with Teri. Everybody in the kitchen was watching him anxiously.

"I am Arcady Mystikos," the man said. "I was taking a nap just a few moments ago. I had a very clear dream. You were in my dream. I saw your name very clearly. And I could tell that you were very curious about me. You wanted to know all about me. When I woke up, I knew I had to get in touch with you right away. We must meet one another."

"How did you get my phone number?" Alex asked, wondering if Mr. Mystikos had dreamed that, too.

Mr. Mystikos laughed a deep laugh. "It was in the phone book."

"Oh," Alex said sheepishly.

"We must meet," Mr. Mystikos said. "I sense that mysterious forces are drawing us together."

"Why are they doing that?" Alex asked.

"Some things we must not question," Mr. Mystikos told him. "Some things we just have to accept."

"Why?" Alex asked.

Mr. Mystikos laughed that deep laugh again. "Oh, Alexander," he said. "I can sense that you are a skeptical one. That is excellent. I know that you have a sharp mind. Bright young people like yourself are always looking for answers. Let us get together and talk. Maybe we can find some answers together—if you are prepared to be open-minded."

"I'm *always* open-minded," Alex said. It irritated him that he had to keep correcting people on that point. "Where should we meet? At my place?"

"I have been invited to a party tomorrow, and I must be fully rested," Mr. Mystikos explained. "I want to demonstrate my special mental gifts. I will not be at my best if I have to run all around town today."

"I see," Alex said.

"Can you stop by my hotel?" Mr. Mystikos asked.

"Can I bring a few friends?" Alex asked.

"Of course," Mr. Mystikos replied. "I look forward to seeing young Mr. Fitzwater again."

Alex stared in surprise at Spencer Fitzwater. How had Mr. Mystikos known that Fitzwater was there with him?

"What's wrong?" asked Fitzwater, who couldn't hear the other side of Alex's conversation.

Alex gave Fitzwater a puzzled look. He wasn't sure what to think about Mr. Mystikos now. Maybe this guy was the real thing. Just because psychic powers aren't likely doesn't mean they are impossible. Alex began to feel a kind of nervous excitement. "Can you meet me here at five o'clock?" Mr. Mystikos asked.

"Sure," Alex said. "Where are you staying?"

"Oh, you don't know the address," Mr. Mystikos said. "I sometimes forget that other people do not have my extra sense. Let me tell you, then. I am staying at the Waterfront Inn, Room 1212."

Alex jotted it down in his notepad. "Okay," he said. "I'll see you there at five o'clock."

"Excellent," Mr. Mystikos said. And just like that, he hung up. Alex found himself listening to the steady drone of the dial tone.

He hung up and looked curiously at Fitzwater. "Mr. Mystikos wants to meet us," he said.

"Who is this guy?" Mrs. Fox asked suspiciously. "Is this safe? I don't want you going anywhere with some stranger, Alex. You never know what could happen."

"You can come along if you want," he told her. "Anyway, we need a ride."

"Good," she said. "That gives me an excuse not to cook. We'll leave your dad a note telling him it's his night to do dinner."

"Wait. I'm getting a psychic flash," Alex said, putting his hand to his forehead. "I predict—I predict we're going to be eating pizza again."

"Mm-hmm," his mother said. "I'll leave your father the number for the pizza place."

Alex looked around for the phone book. That had reminded him of something he'd been wondering about earlier. He picked up the heavy book and began flipping through the white pages. He ran his finger down a long column of names until he got to the listing for his own family.

"What are you doing?" Jay asked, reading over Alex's shoulder. "Don't you know your own phone number?"

"Mr. Mystikos told me he got my number from the phone book, but my name's not even in here," Alex said. "It just has Dad's name. There are a bunch of people named Fox. How did he know which house to call?"

"Duh!" Fitzwater said. "He's a psychic, dummy. He knows everything."

Alex narrowed his eyes. There were definitely some things about this case that were not going to be enjoyable. Hanging around with Spencer Fitzwater was one of them.

Alex was relieved that his mother had decided to stay in the hotel lobby. True, his mother was a science teacher and tended to think about things pretty much the same way Alex did. But she was still his mother. And mothers all seemed to have a special knack for saying things that embarrassed their children.

If Alex believed in any sort of psychic ability whatsoever, it was the ability all mothers seemed to have to predict exactly the most embarrassing things to say about their kids. So he didn't object when his mom volunteered to stay in the lobby and read a magazine while he met upstairs with the mysterious Mr. Mystikos.

Alex, Jay, Teri, and Fitzwater took the elevator to the

twelfth floor. There they found the door bearing the brass number *1212*. Alex exchanged uncertain glances with his companions. None of them knew what to expect.

Alex gathered up his nerve and raised his hand. But before he could even knock, the door opened.

"I know, I know," said the big, dark-haired man standing in the doorway. He sounded bored as he waved them in. "Come in and sit down."

He then turned his back on them and shuffled over to a large, comfortable-looking chair. He slumped into it.

Alex and his crew looked from one person to another. Teri shrugged. Alex decided to go in. There was no sense in going this far and then quitting just because their psychic didn't have the best manners in the world.

Alex entered the room. The others followed quietly. Jay closed the door.

Alex moved hesitantly to a chair facing Mr. Mystikos. He looked around. The hotel room was an impressive one. In fact, it was several rooms. The large room they were standing in was furnished like a living room. Next to it was another room that looked like a bedroom. Alex wasn't sure what a big place like that would cost to stay in, but apparently Mr. Mystikos wasn't hurting for money.

Alex sat down. He studied Mr. Mystikos.

Mr. Mystikos was big. Not exactly fat, just big. And his face was framed by a thick fringe of dark hair and a bushy beard that reminded Alex of a lion's mane. He had an eerie stare, too.

Mr. Mystikos fixed that stare on Alex.

"You are thinking that I am rude," the man grumbled. "I apologize if I sometimes skip the usual greetings. It is just that when one sees the present and the future at the same time, it is easy to jump ahead."

Alex nodded as if this was a problem that anyone might have.

Mr. Mystikos looked up at Jay, Teri, and Fitzwater. They were all gathered around Alex's chair. Mr. Mystikos gestured toward a sofa. "Sit."

They all sat immediately, like frightened puppies.

Mr. Mystikos set his dark eyes on Teri. He stared a moment. Then he said, "Oh, I'm sorry."

"Huh?" she said, apparently figuring that she had missed some part of the conversation.

"I'm sorry," he repeated in his thick accent. "I see that you have recently experienced some hardship, some loss."

"Oh!" she said, as if it all made sense to her now. "My goldfish!"

"Yes, the poor goldfish," Mr. Mystikos said. "It died."

Teri nodded excitedly. "Yes, that's right. The small one. It died last week. How did you know?"

The big man shrugged. "These things just pop into my head. I cannot control it."

"That's amazing," Teri said.

Alex squirmed uneasily in his chair. He sometimes wondered if it did more harm than good to bring Teri along on these investigations. After all, she seemed to accept anything that appealed to her belief in "psychic energy."

Teri usually skipped the part of the investigation where you were supposed to study the facts, come up with a theory that fits the facts, and then test your theory. She jumped right to the part where you accept the theory as fact and start trying to convince others that it's true. Evidence and tests, however, were what separated good theories from bad ones.

Alex pulled out his business card. He started to hand it to Mr. Mystikos, but the big man waved it away.

"I have seen it already," Mr. Mystikos said, pointing to his head. "Up here."

Alex was not exactly convinced that Mr. Mystikos had seen his business card in some sort of dream, but he put it back in his pocket anyway. He pulled out his notebook and pencil.

"What am I thinking?" he asked the psychic.

"You are wondering why I asked you to come here," Mr. Mystikos said without even hesitating.

Alex cocked his head to one side. This was true, but it was also a pretty safe guess. Anyone in Alex's situation would be curious.

"You have doubts," Mr. Mystikos said. "But you also want to know more about me. That is good. As long as you are willing to ask questions, you are open to new ideas. I warn you, though. You might not get the answers you want."

"Oh?" Alex said.

"You expect everything to have a scientific explanation," Mr. Mystikos said. "You think you will find some logical reason for the strange things you have heard about me. But science cannot explain what is outside the range of its instruments. The human mind can tap into energies that scientists cannot yet measure or explain. The universe is a much more wonderful and complex thing than you can even imagine, my young friend."

"Exactly," Teri said. "I keep trying to tell him that, but he won't listen."

Alex rolled his eyes.

"See?" Teri said. "Did you see that look he just made?"

Mr. Mystikos laughed that deep, rich laugh of his. "Young lady, we will try to open his mind together."

Alex sat up with a start. "What's her name?" he demanded, pointing at Teri.

Mr. Mystikos looked at Alex and cocked his eyebrows as if he hadn't heard the question.

"You just called her 'young lady,'" Alex said. "Do you know what her name is?"

Mr. Mystikos turned his attention back to Teri. He stroked his beard thoughtfully while he studied her.

"Some things come to me slowly," he said. "They come to me in pieces. I must put them together like a jigsaw puzzle."

Alex waited impatiently for Mr. Mystikos to sort out his mental "puzzle pieces." Alex had heard similar mumbo jumbo from other people who claimed to have amazing abilities. Usually, it just meant that they were stalling for time.

Jay and Fitzwater hadn't said a word yet. They were apparently waiting anxiously to see if Mr. Mystikos really could read Teri's mind.

The big man closed his eyes. He placed his hand to his forehead. "I see a letter," he announced.

Alex waited for something a little more specific. *Anybody* could predict that a person's name had a letter in it! The question was, could he guess the right letter?

"I see the letter *T*," Mr. Mystikos said.

Teri gasped. "That's right!" she said. "My name is Teri."

Alex rose halfway out of his seat. He wanted to strangle his sister. She had just given Mr. Mystikos the answer. Now there was no way of knowing if this so-called psychic would have been able to guess her name. Alex forced himself to sit down again.

"Yes, Teri!" Mr. Mystikos said triumphantly. "That is exactly the name I see."

Agitated now, Alex tapped his pencil noisily against his notebook. "When is her birthday?" he asked.

Mr. Mystikos swiped his hand though the air. "Questions, questions! I can answer all of your questions in good time, I assure you. But first let me ask *you* a few very important questions, Alexander Fox."

"Such as?" Alex said.

"Do you know everything, my young friend?" Mr. Mystikos asked.

Alex shook his head. "Nobody knows everything."

"Then why are you so unwilling to believe?" Mr. Mystikos asked. "I hate to see so much negative thinking in a person so young. Your mind should be open to new things, new ideas. You should explore the wonderful mysteries of life."

Alex took a deep breath, preparing to deliver his usual speech in defense of a little healthy skepticism. "Skepticism...," he said. But the big man waved him off.

"I will now remove all doubts," Mr. Mystikos said confidently. "Scientists demand evidence. I will give you concrete evidence."

Alex nodded. He couldn't argue against the need for evidence.

Mr. Mystikos reached into a pocket of his fancy silk robe and pulled something out. He leaned forward, holding a small blue pack in front of Alex. It was a deck of playing cards.

"I will flip through these cards," he told Alex. "Stick your finger in anywhere."

He then began flipping through the cards. About halfway through the deck, Alex stuck his finger in.

"Take the card your finger is on," Mr. Mystikos instructed.

Alex did. He looked at it, being careful not to let Mr. Mystikos catch a peek. It was the two of hearts.

"Can you guess what it is?" Fitzwater asked.

"I don't have to guess," Mr. Mystikos said, leaning back in his chair. "I knew before you arrived which card you would pick."

"Oh?" Alex said.

"Yes, I wrote it down," Mr. Mystikos said. "Teri, please open that envelope on the table beside you."

Teri looked curiously at a plain white envelope laying next to the lamp on the table. She started to pick it up, but then Alex hurried over and took it.

"If you don't mind, I'll open it," he said. He didn't want his sister opening something that might be part of a trick.

Mr. Mystikos nodded.

Alex turned the envelope over in his hand, examining it. It looked like a normal envelope. Anyway, Mr. Mystikos hadn't touched it since they'd come in the room. Alex couldn't imagine any way that Mr. Mystikos could have put something inside it while they were talking.

Alex carefully opened one end of the envelope and looked inside. There was a slip of paper in it. He pulled the paper out and read it. Printed on it in neat handwriting were the words "two of hearts."

Alex looked again at the card in his hand. He looked at Mr. Mystikos. A cold tingle ran through his body. He was getting goose bumps all down his arms.

The big man smiled. "Now do you believe?" he asked.

Jay, Teri, and Fitzwater had all crowded around Alex. They read the slip of paper for themselves.

"Wow," Teri said in a stunned whisper.

Alex didn't know what to say. He sat down and thought a moment. He looked around for the deck of cards, but Mr. Mystikos's hands were now empty. He had apparently slipped the deck back in his pocket.

"Can we try that trick again?" Alex asked.

"You see with your own eyes, but still you do not believe," Mr. Mystikos said.

"I believe," Teri assured him.

"So do I," Fitzwater chimed in.

Alex looked at Jay.

Jay shrugged sheepishly. "Well, it is pretty convincing," he said.

"I'd still like to see it again," Alex said.

Mr. Mystikos put his hands over his face. "I am growing weary," he said. "Keeping my senses at such a high level is a great strain on me. I am sorry, but I must ask you to leave now. I must get some rest before the party tomorrow."

"Where is this party going to be?" Alex asked.

"At Mrs. Winslow's," Mr. Mystikos said. "She wants to introduce me to some friends of hers. They have heard about my special mental gifts and are curious to see for themselves."

"I don't want to seem rude," Alex said, "but would it be all right if I came, too? I'd like to see more of your 'special gifts' in action."

The big man laughed. "Still skeptical? Very well. You may come. Be there at seven o'clock. I am sure that by the end of the evening your view of psychic abilities will be quite different."

"I'll come with an open mind," Alex assured him.

"**A**lex!" Don Bogdanski said with a big smile. "Long time no see."

Alex closed the front door to Don's Mighty Magic Shop behind him. He walked over to the glass counter where Don was sorting colorful silk squares.

Stage magicians sometimes used the silks in tricks. Don had once taught Alex how to change one red silk and one white silk into a white silk covered with red polka dots. It was a trick that had impressed all of Alex's friends. And it had only cost him $7.95.

"I've been pretty busy, what with school and all," Alex said.

"What happened with that kid who claimed he could

make salt shakers move without touching them?" Don asked.

"You were right," Alex said. "He was using a thin piece of thread. You could hardly see it."

Don nodded. "I've heard about fake psychics in Russia who have used that trick."

"Have you heard of some guy who calls himself Arcady Mystikos?" Alex asked. "I just met him. He claims to have psychic abilities."

Don shook his head. "Never heard of him. Is he one of those TV psychics?"

"He probably has his own psychic hot line," Alex joked. "You know: 'Call now and I will predict your shoe size! Only $3.95 a minute.'"

Don smiled. "So what's this guy's angle?"

"He says he can read minds," Alex explained. "He's been hanging around with some of the rich folks in town, impressing them with stuff like telling them how many kids they have and finding lost watches for them."

Don nodded. "After he's impressed them with the free stuff, they probably beg him to do a psychic reading for them. He then charges them an arm and a leg to tell them some vague stuff about how they'll be hearing soon from an old friend."

"I have to admit, he's done some things that I can't explain," Alex told him. "I met him last night, and I can't tell if he's using tricks or some kind of real psychic power."

"And I predict that's why you've come to see me," Don said.

Alex smiled. "Exactly."

Don leaned against the counter. "So what's this guy's best trick?"

"He had me pull a card from a deck," Alex said. "Then he told me to open an envelope. I inspected it. It looked like an ordinary envelope. Inside was a slip of paper with the name of the card written on it. That was pretty spooky."

"It wouldn't have been as spooky if he'd let you inspect the deck of cards," Don said. "It's the deck that's the key."

"What do you mean?" Alex asked.

"He used a deck of trick cards," Don explained. "He was able to force you to pick the card he wanted. I could teach you to do that trick in five minutes. But first you'd have to buy the deck."

Alex took out his notebook and jotted that down. "Trick cards."

"What else did he do?" Don asked.

Alex read him the notes about the time Mr. Mystikos had predicted the number that Spencer Fitzwater had written down.

"If you'd let me use my own pad of paper, I could do that one, too," Don said. "In fact, I could teach you to do that trick for just $12.95."

"Let me guess," Alex said. "Trick pad?"

Don smiled. "You're catching on," he said. "If you're dealing with a magician or a cheat, things aren't always what they seem."

"So far, Mr. Mystikos hasn't done anything that a good magician couldn't do," Alex said.

Don nodded. "It's best to rule out tricks before you start believing in real psychic abilities."

"If he is a fake, how can I catch him in the act?" Alex asked.

"Might be easier said than done," Don told him. "Guys like him know a hundred different tricks. You can't tell ahead of time which one he'll be doing next. And if you ask him to try a certain type of prediction under conditions that would keep him from cheating, he'll come up with some sort of excuse why he can't do it just then."

"I asked him to repeat his card trick, and he told me he had to rest," Alex said.

Don nodded. "A good magician never does a trick twice. That way, you can't spot how he's fooling you."

"So, is there any way I can test this guy for psychic abilities?" Alex asked. "I mean a real test, one where he can't cheat."

"It's hard to get people like Mystikos to agree to a real test," Don said. "He doesn't want to get caught cheating!"

"Well, can you at least teach me to do some of his tricks?" Alex asked.

Don gave him a wink. "Sure I can. And I'll give you a real good deal on a deck of trick cards."

Alex had never been to the Fitzwaters' house before. It was huge. Alex hated to think how long it would take to mow that whole lawn. Of course, the Fitzwaters probably didn't mow their own lawn. They would just pay somebody to do it for them.

He rang the bell. He thought a maid or a butler might open the door, but Spencer Fitzwater was the one who answered it.

"Come in, Fox," Fitzwater said. Then he looked Alex up and down. "Is that what you're wearing to the party?"

Alex looked down at his jacket and slacks. His mother had made him put them on after he'd tried to leave the house dressed in his jeans.

"What's wrong with this?" he asked.

Fitzwater sniffed. "Whatever."

Alex stepped inside. He had to admit that Fitzwater's suit looked pretty expensive. It was probably some fancy designer label.

"Where are your 'business associates'?" Fitzwater asked.

"They had homework to do," Alex said.

He wasn't telling the whole truth. In fact, he didn't want to bring Jay and Teri along because they seemed a little too eager to believe everything Mr. Mystikos said. And Alex was afraid that Mr. Mystikos was using that to his advantage.

As for Spencer Fitzwater, Alex would just have to put up with him. After all, the Fitzwaters were the ones giving Alex a ride to the party.

Fitzwater started walking into the next room. "Want something to drink?" he asked over his shoulder.

Alex followed him, looking around curiously at the Fitzwaters' house. They walked through several fancy-looking rooms. Everything looked very expensive. Very tidy and orderly, too. But Alex noticed there weren't any books around.

Alex's home was full of books. Everybody in his family loved to read. He found it hard to believe that people could find ways to amuse themselves without having a good book to read.

Fitzwater led him into a kitchen twice as big as the one in Alex's house. Fitzwater opened the refrigerator. "Soda?" he asked.

"Okay," Alex said, looking around the kitchen. His eyes stopped on the answering machine, moved down the counter, and then returned to the answering machine.

"Did you call home before you came to my house yesterday?" he asked.

"Yeah," Fitzwater said. "Why?"

"Would your message still be on there?" Alex asked, pointing to the answering machine.

"Maybe," Fitzwater said, coming over with two cans of soda. "If my mom saved it."

"Let's see if it's still on there," Alex suggested.

Fitzwater looked puzzled, but he handed the cold cans to Alex and then pushed a button on the answering machine. The tape rewound and then stopped with a click. Fitzwater's voice came from the machine as it started to replay his message.

"Hi, Mom," it said. "This is Scooter."

Alex looked at Fitzwater. "Scooter?"

"Shut up," Fitzwater snapped. Apparently, he had a family nickname that nobody at school knew about. Alex grinned.

"I'm at school," the message continued. "I'm going to visit this kid named Fox. I told him about Mr. Mystikos, and he wants to 'investigate.' He even has his own business card. It says, 'Alexander Fox, scientific investigator.' Isn't that a laugh?"

Alex looked at Fitzwater.

Fitzwater just shrugged.

"Here's his number," said the voice on the machine, and it read off Alex's phone number. That was pretty much the end of the message.

Fitzwater studied Alex. "Why did you want to hear that?" he asked.

"I'll explain in a minute," Alex said. "Where are your parents?"

"Upstairs," Fitzwater said. "We were just waiting for you to show up."

"Let's get them and head to the party," Alex suggested.

"Don't you even want your drink?" Fitzwater asked him.

"I'll get something at the party," Alex said. He opened the fridge and put the two cans back. He was now dying to ask Fitzwater's mother a few questions.

Fitzwater led him back to the front door. Mr. and Mrs. Fitzwater were heading down the stairs as they entered. Now Alex really did feel underdressed. Mrs. Fitzwater was wearing an expensive-looking black-beaded gown, and Mr. Fitzwater had on a tuxedo.

Alex nervously straightened his tie.

"Hello, Mr. and Mrs. Fitzwater," he said.

"You must be Alex," Mrs. Fitzwater said with a warm smile. "Nice to meet you."

She didn't sound as snooty and stuck-up as Alex had expected. Maybe Spencer and his two brothers were more spoiled than their parents.

"You're the boy who doesn't believe anything?" Mr. Fitzwater said.

Alex tried not to lose his cool. "I'm a scientific investigator," he explained. "I don't believe unlikely claims until they've been tested. That's the scientific method."

"Well, just don't do anything to embarrass us tonight," Mr. Fitzwater warned him. "I'm not even sure why Mr. Mystikos would invite a couple of kids to this kind of party."

Alex decided not to argue. But he wasn't sure he liked Mr. Fitzwater. Apparently, Spencer was more like his father than his mother.

"At first, I was skeptical about Mr. Mystikos, too," Mrs. Fitzwater told Alex. "But then I saw him do some of the most amazing things. He convinced my husband, too."

"Mrs. Fitzwater, was Mr. Mystikos here yesterday?" Alex asked.

"Yes, he was," she said. "I asked him to come over and give me a personal psychic reading."

"Was he in the kitchen with you when you listened to the message from Scoot...I mean, Spencer?" Alex asked.

Spencer Fitzwater shot him a nasty look.

"I believe he was," she replied. "Scooter had..."

"Mom!" Spencer whined.

"Oh, I'm sorry, dear," she said. "*Spencer* had apparently called while Mr. Mystikos was giving me my reading. We listened to the message afterward. Then Mr. Mystikos had to go back to his hotel to rest. It's very tiring being a psychic, you know."

Alex took out his notebook and began writing.

"What's all this about?" Spencer Fitzwater asked.

"I was wondering how Mr. Mystikos knew so much about me when he called my house," Alex explained. "But it was all there on your message. You read him everything on my business card. He just had to remember the phone number."

Mrs. Fitzwater laughed. "Mr. Mystikos does not have to eavesdrop on other people's phone messages," she said. "I assure you, he does have genuine psychic abilities. He told me things about myself that were so true it was chilling."

"Well, we'll see about that," Alex said. "We'll see."

Spencer Fitzwater had been right. The Winslows did have more money than the Fitzwaters. The Winslows' house was BIG. And the door was answered by a real butler.

Entering the mansion, Alex looked around at all the expensive furniture and works of art. It was no mystery why Mr. Mystikos liked to hang around with people like the Fitzwaters and the Winslows. These people had a lot of money to throw around on things like psychic readings. And they had lots of friends who were just as rich. These dinner parties were a great place for Mr. Mystikos to line up new customers.

Mrs. Winslow greeted them in the living room. She

was an elegant-looking woman with graying hair. She shook Alex's hand with a smile. "Pleased to meet you," she said. "Mr. Mystikos told me that you'd be our guest tonight. Delighted to have you here."

"Thank you, ma'am," Alex said uneasily.

She was being so nice to him that he felt kind of guilty about being there to test Mr. Mystikos's psychic powers. He didn't want to ruin her party. Still, he reminded himself that Mr. Mystikos had agreed to let him come. And Alex also figured he would be saving Mrs. Winslow and her friends a lot of money if he found out that Mr. Mystikos was tricking them.

"Is Mr. Mystikos here?" Alex asked.

"Not yet," Mrs. Winslow said. "I hope he didn't…" But before she could even finish her sentence, Mr. Mystikos entered with his arms thrown out in a dramatic gesture.

"Good evening, my friends," he said in a booming voice. He was dressed in a tuxedo with a black cape. Some sort of large, odd-looking charm was hanging from a gold chain around his neck. He looked well-dressed, and yet somewhat strange and mysterious.

Everyone in the room turned to look at him. Alex had to admit that Mr. Mystikos had a talent for getting noticed. Alex had a feeling that Mr. Mystikos would always find some way to make himself the center of attention in any group.

Mr. Mystikos whipped off the cape and handed it to the butler. He then marched across the Oriental rug and took Mrs. Winslow's hand in his. He gave her hand a kiss.

"Mrs. Winslow," he said. "As charming as always."

Her cheeks blushed a rosy red as she laughed.

Mr. Mystikos eyed Alex. "Ah, the young skeptic," he said. "Glad you could make it. Tonight I intend to remove any doubts you might have about my psychic abilities."

"I'd be quite happy about that," Alex said. "Maybe we can arrange a test."

Mr. Mystikos apparently hadn't heard that last part. He turned his back on Alex and started talking to a woman with long, blonde hair. The other guests were gathering curiously around the psychic. Mrs. Winslow began introducing them all to Mr. Mystikos. Alex wanted to ask Mr. Mystikos some more questions, but Mrs. Winslow started telling everyone about the wonderful things Mr. Mystikos had seen in her future during a recent psychic reading.

It was obvious that Mrs. Winslow believed everything the psychic told her. Alex began to wonder if that kind of trust might not be dangerous in certain situations. After all, who really knew anything about this stranger? Alex didn't even know if the man really was from Greece. For all he knew, the guy could be some con man with a fake accent. If so, who knew how much money he might try to trick Mrs. Winslow out of?

Spencer Fitzwater didn't seem very interested in the adults' conversation. He roamed around the room, poking around in drawers that he had no business opening.

Alex stayed close to Mrs. Winslow and Mr. Mystikos,

listening to every word. Mr. Mystikos told each guest some little fact about themselves. For instance, he knew that Mr. Marshall drove a Mercedes. And he knew that Mrs. Clairedale's favorite color was red. Of course, she was wearing a bright red dress, so it didn't take psychic abilities to come up with that one.

Some of the guests seemed a bit skeptical about Mr. Mystikos's ESP at first, but Alex noticed them smiling and nodding as the psychic continued to make his little observations.

After half an hour or so of this psychic chitchat, Mr. Mystikos excused himself to use the rest room. When he returned, everyone moved to the dining room to eat a late dinner.

The food was wonderful, as good as anything Alex had ever had in a restaurant. Neither of his parents could cook like that. The chicken was smothered with some kind of sauce that Alex didn't know the name of. If the main dish was that good, Alex wondered what the dessert would be like. He hoped it would be chocolate mousse.

Chocolate mousse was like pudding, but better. He'd had it a few times in restaurants. Alex began to feel guilty now about not inviting Teri. She loved chocolate mousse just as much as he did.

Unfortunately, they never got to the dessert. In the middle of the meal, Mrs. Winslow suddenly jumped out of her chair. "My ring!" she cried, staring at her hand. "My ring is missing!"

A fuss broke out around the table as everybody

started asking what the ring looked like and what could have happened to it and where was it last seen.

Then somebody suggested that maybe Mr. Mystikos was the one to ask.

Mr. Mystikos wiped his mouth with a linen napkin, rose to his feet, and held up a reassuring hand. "Never fear," he said. "I will do everything in my power to locate this missing ring."

Mrs. Winslow looked relieved. "What do we need to do?" she asked.

"I will need another object that you have worn recently," Mr. Mystikos explained. "Because they have both been in close contact with you, the vibrations of one will be in tune with the vibrations of the other. If I can focus on those vibrations, they will lead me to your ring."

Mrs. Winslow nodded as if this made perfect sense. But it sounded like a lot of mumbo jumbo to Alex.

Mr. Mystikos readied himself. He took off his jacket and draped it over the chair. He then rolled up his shirt sleeves.

Alex watched carefully as Mr. Mystikos took a bracelet from Mrs. Winslow. The big man placed both hands around the bracelet and closed his eyes. He rubbed his fingers over it. He turned to the right. He hesitated. He turned to his left. He turned back to his right. Then he began walking slowly.

Mr. Mystikos didn't travel in a straight line. Rather, he wandered along a crooked path, mumbling to himself. Everyone else followed him curiously. No one dared to speak.

They followed him into a big room. Every now and then, Mr. Mystikos would stop and touch something in the room, like a lamp or a vase. But he would just shake his head and move on.

"This is how he found my mom's watch," Spencer Fitzwater whispered to Alex.

Alex nodded, but he didn't take his eyes off the psychic. A good investigator didn't let himself get distracted.

The whole group moved quietly into the area near the front door. Mr. Mystikos started up the stairs. "Ah," he said. "We are getting closer. I can feel the ring's presence now."

Mrs. Winslow looked excited by this news, but she did not say anything.

Everyone tiptoed up the stairs behind the psychic.

Mr. Mystikos paused at the top of the stairs, turning uncertainly first this way and then that. Apparently feeling some sort of mental tug that no one else could feel, he started down the hall to his right.

He went past a door, then turned and went back to it. He rubbed the bracelet some more and then went inside. A dozen guests followed behind him.

In the room, Alex saw a bed and a dresser and some other furniture that one might expect to find in a bedroom. But there was nothing personal, like clothes or family photos. Alex figured it was a guest room.

"We are getting closer," Mr. Mystikos informed his audience. "I can feel it. We are getting quite close now. Ring, ring, where are you?"

He turned in a slow circle, holding the bracelet out as if it were a compass. Then, dramatically, he pointed to the dresser. "There!" he cried. "Look in there, Mrs. Winslow."

Mrs. Winslow went quickly to the dresser and opened the top drawer. With a gasp, she reached in and pulled out her diamond ring. Her hands were shaking as she slipped the ring back on her finger.

"Oh, my goodness," she said. "How did it ever get up here? I haven't been in this room all week."

"I must apologize," Mr. Mystikos said. "It is all my fault."

Alex looked up at the big man.

"Whenever I am around, strange things happen," Mr. Mystikos said. "Objects just appear and disappear without warning. I think I must be surrounded by some strange energy that causes objects to move from place to place. It is very unsettling, I know. I apologize."

Everyone began talking at once. The whole crowd was amazed by these strange events. Certainly, none of them had ever heard of someone who could cause objects to move around a house.

"See?" Spencer Fitzwater said, nudging Alex with his elbow. "I told you he could find lost objects."

"It is a bit crowded in here," Mr. Mystikos said. "Let us return to the dining room, my friends."

Still talking about the ring, everyone followed him into the hall. Alex and Fitzwater went out last.

"I can think of at least one reason why that ring might have turned up in the guest room," Alex said in a low voice. "And it doesn't involve psychic abilities."

"What do you mean?" Fitzwater asked.

Alex pointed to the door right across the hall from the guest room. Inside was a bathroom.

"Mr. Mystikos excused himself to use the rest room before dinner," he explained. "It's possible that he ducked into the guest room just long enough to plant that ring in the dresser."

Fitzwater rolled his eyes. "And how did he get the ring in the first place, Mr. Know-it-all?" he asked.

"Well, I do remember him taking Mrs. Winslow's hand and kissing it," Alex said. "Any good pickpocket or stage magician could have slipped the ring off without her noticing it. I once saw a magician on TV slip off a guy's watch and suspenders without him even realizing what was going on."

"Mr. Mystikos is not a pickpocket," Fitzwater insisted.

"How do you know?" Alex asked. "Can you read minds, too?"

Looking disgusted, Fitzwater hurried to catch up with the others.

Everybody returned to the dining room, but unfortunately the other guests were too excited to think about eating dessert. Instead, they insisted on seeing Mr. Mystikos demonstrate more of his amazing abilities.

Mr. Mystikos seemed reluctant at first, but he quickly gave in. "Very well," he said. "I cannot guarantee success, though. Psychic abilities are not something you can turn on and off like a light switch. They come and go as they please. If everybody keeps an open mind and keeps negative thoughts out of this room, I believe we can do some amazing things together."

Everyone gathered around him, looking quite excited about the idea of witnessing actual psychic abilities at work.

Mr. Mystikos took some things out of the pocket of his jacket, which was still draped over his chair.

Alex took out his notebook.

“**W**e might be more comfortable in the living room,” Mr. Mystikos suggested.

Everybody followed Mr. Mystikos back to the living room. They all gathered around him, expecting great things.

Mr. Mystikos held up a pad of paper. He tore off the top sheet and looked around the group. His eyes settled on Alex.

“I’d like my curious young friend to help me in this experiment,” Mr. Mystikos said. He handed the paper and pen to Alex.

“Write down any number from one to a hundred,” he told Alex.

Alex studied the piece of paper. Based on Spencer Fitzwater's description of this trick, he had expected Mr. Mystikos to hand him the entire pad. Instead, Alex was holding only one sheet. Maybe Mr. Mystikos was planning to do a different trick this time.

Alex turned his back and wrote down the number $16\frac{1}{2}$. He had decided to make things difficult for Mr. Mystikos.

He folded the paper twice and turned around.

"Let's orient you better," Mr. Mystikos said. "I've found that facing north often helps me keep my senses sharp. Maybe it has something to do with aligning myself with the Earth's magnetic field. I don't know. Anyway, let's position you like this."

He took hold of Alex's shoulders and turned him slightly, so Alex was facing to the north.

"Can you feel the difference?" the psychic asked.

Alex was a little confused by all of this. Before he could even answer, Mr. Mystikos took the folded slip of paper from him.

The psychic walked over to a glass ash tray, dropped the paper in it, and then pulled a pack of matches from his pants pocket. Everyone watched in surprise as Mr. Mystikos lit the match and set fire to the paper. It was gone in an instant, turned to black ash.

"We won't need that anymore," he said. "The number is now in Alex's head, and it will soon be in my head."

He turned and fixed his dark eyes on Alex. "You must help me," he said. "You must concentrate with me. Keep only positive thoughts in your head. We must work together. We must feel the energy together. We must succeed together."

Alex nodded, just to make everyone happy.

"Concentrate," the psychic urged him. "Concentrate."

Alex pretended he was concentrating.

Mr. Mystikos wandered around the room, touching his forehead. "I'm sensing it now," he told everyone. "I'm definitely sensing it."

Everyone waited in silent anticipation.

Mr. Mystikos turned to face a corner opposite Alex. He put his head down. "I see a number," he announced. "I see two numbers."

He paused. "Wait," he said. "I see four numbers. I'm confused. How can there be four numbers? But, yes, I definitely see four numbers. I see a one, a six, a one, and a two. But how could your number be 1612?"

Suddenly, the psychic spun around. He pointed toward the heavens. "I have it!" he declared. "Your number is sixteen-and-a-half!"

Everyone looked at Alex.

Alex nodded sheepishly. "That's right," he said.

Everyone gasped. Then they clapped. The group broke into excited chatter.

Mr. Mystikos laughed that deep laugh of his. "Our young friend tried to trick me, no?" he said. "What do you think of my special gifts now, Alexander Fox?"

Alex hesitated. That was a mind-reading trick he hadn't been prepared for. He had no idea how it was done. It certainly seemed like something that normal human beings could not do. Was it possible that he was actually witnessing something that science could not explain? Could Mr. Mystikos really read minds?

"I think...," Alex said slowly, "I think I'd like to make a phone call."

Mrs. Winslow looked at him curiously. "A phone call?"

"I want to tell my mom that I'll be home later than I thought," he said quickly. "I don't want her to worry. Is there a phone in the kitchen?"

"Yes, dear," Mrs. Winslow said. "You can go straight through the dining room."

Alex headed toward the kitchen. His thoughts were whizzing around and around in his head as if they'd been thrown into a blender. There had to be some good explanation for Mr. Mystikos's latest mind-reading demonstration, but Alex could not think of one. He needed help.

He picked up the phone and dialed Don Bogdanski's number. The magic shop would be closed by now, but Alex knew Don's home number.

Alex waited impatiently while the phone rang on the other end. "Come on," he muttered. "You have to be home."

"Hello?" said Don's voice on the other end.

"It's Alex," said Alex. "I need some expert advice."

"What did he do?" Don asked. "Bend a spoon with his brain waves?"

Alex explained the mind-reading trick, trying to include every detail he could remember. He didn't want to leave out any clue that might tip off an experienced stage magician like Don.

"Mr. Mystikos took the paper from you and then burned it?" Don asked as Alex finished his story.

"Yeah," Alex replied.

"Wait," Don said. "I'm having a psychic flash of my own. I can see a number. I see the number twenty-two."

"Twenty-two?" Alex said, confused.

"Yes, twenty-two," Don said. "Look on page twenty-two of that book I sold you today."

Then he hung up. Any good magician likes to make a quick, dramatic exit, and Don was no exception.

Alex reached into his jacket pocket and pulled out the paperback book he had bought at Don's shop in the morning. It included instructions on how to perform more than fifty mentalist tricks. *Mentalism* was what stage magicians called tricks like mind-reading and predicting what card would be drawn from a deck.

Each page of the book showed that there were no supernatural abilities required. There was some simple explanation for every amazing event. The key was to keep your audience from spotting the way you did the trick. Obviously, Mr. Mystikos was quite good at that. He had gotten Alex so confused with that business about facing north that Alex had missed how the trick had actually been done.

He turned anxiously to page twenty-two in the book. On the facing page was a drawing of a magician holding up a burning slip of paper. Presto! The secret to Mr. Mystikos's amazing trick was right there in Alex's hands.

Alex read the description of the trick, step by step. It matched almost exactly what he had seen Mr. Mystikos do. Alex slapped his head.

"Dummy!" he said to himself. "I let him get his hands on the answer."

He realized now that Mr. Mystikos had switched papers, keeping the one with Alex's answer on it and burning a blank one. Then all he had to do was turn his back and read the answer.

Alex closed the book and walked back into the dining room. He wasn't sure what to do next. He had been hoping that he could do the exact same trick in front of everybody at the party. They would all be amazed that Alex seemed to have psychic powers, too. Then he would explain that he had used a simple magic trick to do exactly what this so-called psychic had just done.

Unfortunately, this particular trick required some sleight of hand, and Alex wasn't very good at that kind of magic. It required a lot of practice to hide something in your hand so nobody could see it. Magicians called it *palming*. If Alex tried to do it, he was sure he'd mess up the trick.

Maybe he should just show everybody page twenty-two in the book. That would mean breaking the magician's rule about not explaining tricks to the audience, but Mr. Mystikos wasn't exactly playing by the rules. Stage magicians with any sense of honor did not claim to have real psychic abilities so they could get paid for doing "psychic readings."

If Mr. Mystikos was doing simple tricks and lying about it, then he wasn't a respectable magician. He was a con artist.

Alex was so deep in thought that he was not watching where he was going. He bumped into the chair that had Mr. Mystikos's jacket draped over it. The chair tipped over.

Embarrassed, Alex bent over to pick it up. It was then that he noticed what had just fallen out of the jacket's pocket.

Alex was struck by an idea. Maybe he *could* test Mr. Mystikos in a way that would not allow cheating. Alex knew that in any good test, the tester had to control the situation, not the person being tested. You had to be able to prevent cheating.

Every time Mr. Mystikos did one of his tricks, he controlled the whole situation. It was hard to tell if he was cheating because he was the only one who knew what was going to happen next. And he never did the same trick twice.

Alex looked cautiously toward the living room. Nobody could see him. He made up his mind to set up his own test for the mysterious Mr. Mystikos.

Alex returned to the living room. He had already put the magic book back in his pocket. There was no sense in tipping off Mr. Mystikos.

Everyone was gathered around Mr. Mystikos like spectators at a carnival sideshow. The psychic was showing them some sort of card trick.

"The two of hearts!" he declared.

Everyone applauded.

Mrs. Fitzwater turned toward Alex. "You missed the most amazing things," she told him. "It's just scary the things that Mr. Mystikos can predict."

Alex just nodded. "Mr. Mystikos," he said. "I was wondering if I could take a look at those cards."

Mr. Mystikos quickly slipped the deck of cards into his pants pocket with one hand and put the other hand on his forehead. "Oh, I feel a bit dizzy," he said. "My friends, I'm afraid all of this concentration is tiring me. I hate to stop, but I must rest for a while."

The others moaned in disappointment, but Mr. Mystikos pushed past them and headed back to the dining room. They all followed.

"I will be staying in town for several more weeks," the psychic told them. "Perhaps we can meet again before I leave."

"I hear that you do personal psychic readings," said Mrs. Clairedale, the woman who liked the color red.

"Occasionally," Mr. Mystikos said. "But they require a great deal of concentration. I find them very tiring."

"I would pay you, of course," Mrs. Clairedale said. "Money is no object."

As tired as Mr. Mystikos claimed to be, he still had the energy to whip out his notepad. He jotted something down and handed it to the eager woman.

"Here is my room number at the hotel, madam," he said. "Give me a call. Perhaps we can arrange a time to meet."

Suddenly, the other guests were all pushing closer. They all wanted to make an appointment for a personal psychic reading. Apparently, Mr. Mystikos had done a good job of advertising his services with his little tricks in the living room. Now everyone wanted him to use his "special gifts" to predict their future.

Alex could understand their curiosity. Every human

being wants to know what good things and bad things might be in store for them. But it upset Alex to see that some people were willing to give their money to a stranger when the existence of "psychic powers" had never even been proven. The things Mr. Mystikos did were impressive, but they were no different from tricks that magicians performed. Alex wanted proof before he would begin to believe that Mr. Mystikos could really read minds and predict the future.

And if Mr. Mystikos could see the future, that raised another question in Alex's mind. Why didn't Mr. Mystikos just predict the next big lottery number and make himself rich? People who call themselves psychics often make a lot of money, but they don't do it by winning lotteries or betting on horse races. Instead, they do it by convincing other people that they can predict the future. Then they charge them a lot of money to make vague predictions about jobs and marriages. Some of them even start telephone hot lines. At least Mr. Mystikos would come to your house in person to take your money.

While Mr. Mystikos was busy handing out his room number, Alex looked wishfully at the dinner table. He was hoping everyone might decide to sit down again and finally get to the dessert. Unfortunately, they all seemed too excited now to think about food. Mr. Mystikos had gotten what he came for: new business. After handing out his room number to all of his new customers, he took his jacket off the chair where he had left it. He slipped it on.

"I'm afraid I must leave you now, my friends," he said. "I hope you will all stay in touch. I think I can help you answer any questions you have about your future."

"I have a question for you," Alex said.

"I will give you my room number," Mr. Mystikos said. "You can call me."

"I already know your room number," Alex reminded the psychic. "But I have a question I think you might want to hear right now."

"Yes?" Mr. Mystikos said, looking a bit suspicious.

Alex smiled a mischievous smile. "Where's the *key* to your hotel room?"

Mr. Mystikos reached into his jacket pocket. "Right here," he said. "I..."

He stopped in midsentence. His hand fished around in his pocket. Then he reached in his other jacket pocket.

He chuckled nervously. He reached in his pants pocket. Then in the other pants pocket.

"I remember now," he said. "I left it at the hotel desk. I will get it when I return."

"It's not at the hotel desk," Alex told him. "It's somewhere in this house."

"Oh, Alex," Mrs. Fitzwater said. "How could you possibly know something like that?"

"Because I hid it," Alex said simply.

Everyone murmured in surprise.

"Hid it?" Mrs. Winslow said, sounding shocked. "What do you mean you hid it?"

Alex looked at them all smugly. He folded his arms.

"It fell out of Mr. Mystikos's pocket when I accidentally knocked his chair over. Then I decided to hide it."

"But why?" Mrs. Winslow asked. "Why would you do something like that?"

"I want to see Mr. Mystikos use his psychic powers to find the key," Alex said. "He's very good at finding things that he hid, but I'd like to see him find something that somebody else hid."

Mr. Mystikos looked outraged. "Well, I never!" he said angrily. "I can't believe what I'm hearing!"

"Prove I'm wrong," Alex said. "Find your hotel key."

Mr. Mystikos glared at Alex. "I'm too tired," he said. "I don't have the strength to use my special powers again tonight."

"I'm not surprised," Alex said. "Your powers only seem to work when you want them to. I have a suggestion, though. I will give you back the key tonight. Then we'll all meet back here tomorrow. I will hide something of yours somewhere in this house. You will use your psychic powers to find it. Is that a fair test of your powers? If you can do that, then I will be convinced that you really are a psychic."

Mr. Mystikos frowned. But then he nodded. "I think you need a good lesson in manners, young man," he said. "But I will agree to meet you here. Then I can prove to everyone that my special gift is real."

"Deal," Alex said. He reached under a dinner plate on the table and pulled out the missing key.

Mr. Mystikos glared at Alex as he took the key back. He then said a hasty goodbye and left.

All of the adults in the room started to talk angrily to Alex. They were all trying to speak at once. It seemed that they thought he had spoiled the evening by being so rude to their guest, Mr. Mystikos.

Alex held up his hand. "I apologize if I spoiled your party," he said. "Let me try to make it up to you by offering a little entertainment of my own. I would like to show you a trick I learned recently."

He reached into his pocket and pulled out a deck of trick cards that he had bought at Don's shop.

"What finally happened with that psychic you were investigating?" Alex's mother asked him several days later.

"He didn't show up at Mrs. Winslow's house the next day," Alex explained. "We called the hotel, but he had already checked out. Mrs. Fitzwater heard from some friends in New York that Mr. Mystikos had gone to show his tricks to some rich people living up there."

"Did you ever prove he was a fake?" his mother asked.

"I didn't have to prove he was a fake," Alex said. "Mr. Mystikos was the one making the big claims. It was up to him to prove that he was the real thing. He refused to take part in a real test, though."

"Sounds like he had something to hide," his mother said.

"He certainly got out of town in a hurry," Alex said.

"Oh, yeah?" Teri said. "Well, if he's not a real psychic, how did he know that my name begins with the letter *T*? Explain that."

"Raise your arm," Alex told his sister.

She did.

Alex pointed to the charm bracelet around her wrist. Dangling between a little silver dog and a heart was the letter *T.*

"It doesn't take an extra sense to see that," he said.